WHITE IS FOR BLUEBERRY

By **George Shannon**

Pictures by **Laura Dronzek**

Greenwillow Books
An Imprint of HarperCollinsPublishers

For all the painters who help me see
—G. S.

For my mother
—L. D.

Library of Congress
Cataloging-in-Publication Data
Shannon, George. White is for blueberry /
by George Shannon ; pictures by Laura Dronzek.
    p. cm.
"Greenwillow Books."

Summary: Encourages the reader to look at objects in nature
from another perspective, observing their colors in a new way.
ISBN 0-06-029275-X (trade). ISBN 0-06-029276-8 (lib. bdg.)
[1. Color—Fiction. 2. Perception—Fiction.]
I. Dronzek, Laura, ill. II. Title. PZ7.S5288Wh 2005
[E]—dc22 2004010147
First Edition 10 9 8 7 6 5 4 3 2 1

 Greenwillow Books

PINK

is for crow . . .

when it has just hatched

from its egg.

BLACK

is

for

poppy . . .

when we take the time

RED

is for leaves . . .

when they are blowing
in an autumn breeze.

GREEN

is for turnip . . .

when we see it in

the farmer's field.

PURPLE

is

for

snow . . .

when the snow is the shadow of us.

WHITE

is for blueberry . . .

when the berry is still

too young to pick.

BLUE

is

for

firelight . . .

when the fire is at the tip
of a candlewick.

YELLOW

is for pine tree . . .

when the tree has been cut
and sawed to build.

BROWN

is for sweet potato . . .

when the potato is
still inside its skin.

ORANGE

is for sky . . .

when the sun

has nearly set.

**It all depends on when we look . . .
how near or far . . .**

outside

or in.